First published 1986 by
Walker Books Ltd
184-192 Drummond Street
London NW1 3HP

First printed 1986
Printed and bound by
L.E.G.O., Vicenza, Italy

British Library Cataloguing in Publication Data
Ormerod, Jan
Our Ollie. – (Little ones)
I. Title   II. Series
823 [J]   PZ7

ISBN 0-7445-0487-2

Our Ollie

Jan Ormerod

WALKER BOOKS
LONDON

Ollie

sleeps like a

cat.

Ollie
yawns like a
hippopotamus.

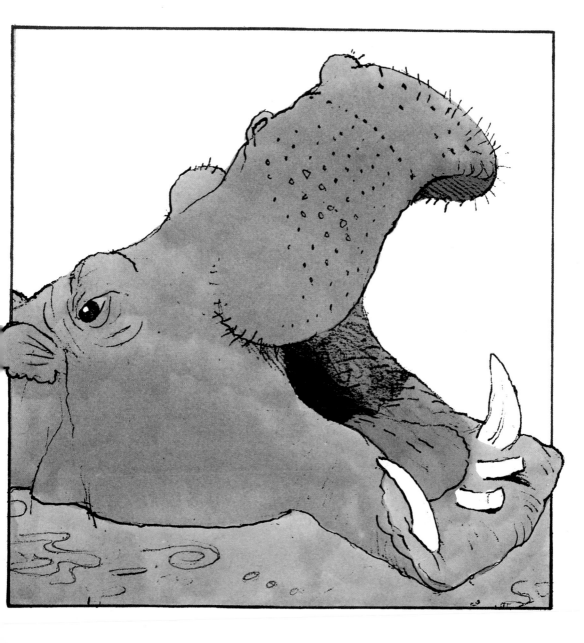

Ollie
crows like a
cockerel.

Ollie
has hair like a
hedgehog's.

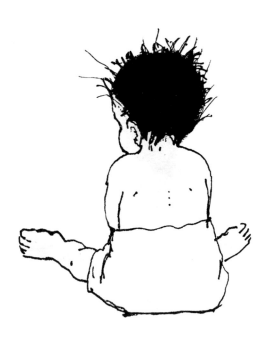

Ollie
is red, blue, green
and yellow like a
parrot.

Ollie
sits like a little frog.

Ollie
hugs like a
bear.

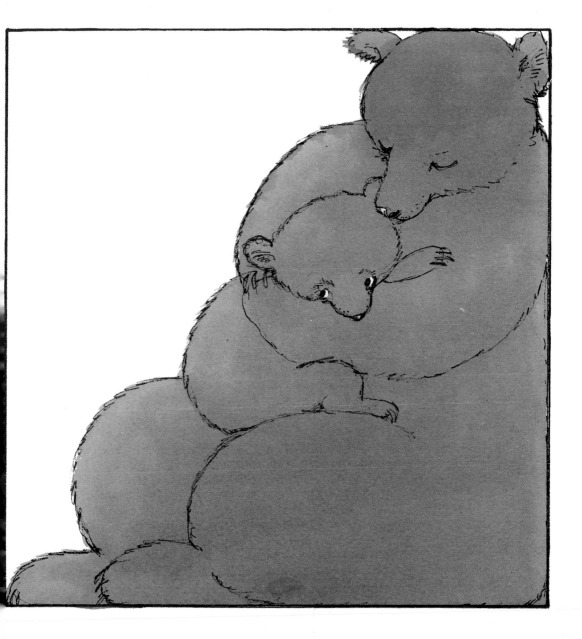

How does Ollie sleep?

How does Ollie yawn?

How does he sound when he crows?

How does his hair look?

How is he dressed?

How does he sit?

How does he hug?

WHO is Ollie?

Ollie is the baby.

He's our Ollie!